Note to parents, carers and teachers

Read it yourself is a series of modern stories, favourite characters and traditional tales written in a simple way for children who are learning to read. The books can be read independently or as part of a guided reading session.

Each book is carefully structured to include many high-frequency words vital for first reading. The sentences on each page are supported closely by pictures to help with understanding, and to offer lively details to talk about.

The books are graded into four levels that progressively introduce wider vocabulary and longer stories as a reader's ability and confidence grows.

Ideas for use

- Begin by looking through the book and talking about the pictures. Has your child heard this story before?

- Help your child with any words he does not know, either by helping him to sound them out or supplying them yourself.

- Developing readers can be concentrating so hard on the words that they sometimes don't fully grasp the meaning of what they're reading. Answering the puzzle questions at the end of the book will help with understanding.

For more information and advice on Read it yourself and book banding, visit www.ladybird.com/readityourself

Book Band 5

Level 1 is ideal for children who have received some initial reading instruction. Each story is told very simply, using a small number of frequently repeated words.

Special features:

chair

Daddy Pig

Peppa

Mummy Pig

Madame Gazelle

jumble sale

Opening pages introduce key story words

Large, clear type

"You can give this old chair, Daddy," says Peppa.

"No. This is a very good chair," says Daddy Pig.

Careful match between story and pictures

Educational Consultant: Geraldine Taylor
Book Banding Consultant: Kate Ruttle

LADYBIRD BOOKS

UK | USA | Canada | Ireland | Australia
India | New Zealand | South Africa

Ladybird Books is part of the Penguin Random House group of companies
whose addresses can be found at global.penguinrandomhouse.com.
www.penguin.co.uk   www.puffin.co.uk   www.ladybird.co.uk

First published 2014
001

This book copyright © ABD Ltd/Ent. One UK Ltd 2014

This book is based on the TV series Peppa Pig.
Peppa Pig is created by Neville Astley and Mark Baker.
Peppa Pig © Astley Baker Davies Ltd/Entertainment One UK Ltd 2003.
www.peppapig.com

Printed in China

A CIP catalogue record for this book is available from the British Library

ISBN: 978–0–241–20491–7

All correspondence to:
Ladybird Books
Penguin Random House Children's
8 Viaduct Gardens, London SW11 7BW

MIX
Paper from
responsible sources
FSC® C018179

Daddy Pig's
Old Chair

Adaptation written by Ellen Philpott
Based on the TV series 'Peppa Pig'. 'Peppa Pig' is created
by Neville Astley and Mark Baker

chair

Peppa

Madame Gazelle

Daddy Pig

Mummy Pig

jumble sale

"We have to buy
a new school roof,"
says Madame Gazelle.
"We will have a jumble
sale to make money."

9

Peppa gives her toys to the jumble sale, to make money.

"I will give this toy, too," says Peppa.

"You can give this old chair, Daddy," says Peppa.

"No. This is a very good chair," says Daddy Pig.

Peppa gives all the toys
to Madame Gazelle.

"You can have this old chair,
too," says Mummy Pig.

15

Peppa, Mummy Pig and Daddy Pig go to the jumble sale. Peppa's friends go, too.

Daddy's chair is at the jumble sale. It looks very old.

19

Peppa looks at all the toys
with her friends. Her old toy
looks very good.

"I will buy my old toy back," says Peppa.

All her friends buy their old toys back, too.

"I will buy this chair," says Daddy. "It will look good with the old one."

"No. It IS the old one!"
says Mummy Pig.

"Oh. It was a lot of money,"
says Daddy Pig.

"Good," says Madame Gazelle. "We have made a lot of money. We can buy a new school roof!"

29

How much do you remember about Peppa Pig: Daddy Pig's Old Chair? Answer these questions and find out!

- **Why is Madame Gazelle having a jumble sale?**

- **What does Peppa take to the jumble sale?**

- **What does Daddy Pig buy at the jumble sale?**

Look at the pictures from the story and say the order they should go in.

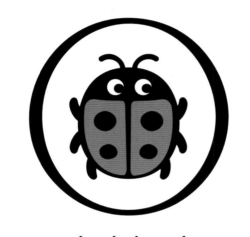

www.ladybird.com